D1503016

Dear Parent:

Congratulations! Your child is taking the first steps on an exciting journey. The destination? Independent reading!

STEP INTO READING® will help your child get there. The program offers books at five levels that accompany children from their first attempts at reading to reading success. Each step includes fun stories, fiction and nonfiction, and colorful art. There are also Step into Reading Sticker Books, Step into Reading Math Readers, and Step into Reading Phonics Readers— a complete literacy program with something to interest every child.

Learning to Read, Step by Step!

Ready to Read   Preschool–Kindergarten
• big type and easy words • rhyme and rhythm • picture clues
For children who know the alphabet and are eager to begin reading.

Reading with Help   Preschool–Grade 1
• basic vocabulary • short sentences • simple stories
For children who recognize familiar words and sound out new words with help.

Reading on Your Own   Grades 1–3
• engaging characters • easy-to-follow plots • popular topics
For children who are ready to read on their own.

Reading Paragraphs   Grades 2–3
• challenging vocabulary • short paragraphs • exciting stories
For newly independent readers who read simple sentences with confidence.

Ready for Chapters   Grades 2–4
• chapters • longer paragraphs • full-color art
For children who want to take the plunge into chapter books but still like colorful pictures.

STEP INTO READING® is designed to give every child a successful reading experience. The grade levels are only guides. Children can progress through the steps at their own speed, developing confidence in their reading, no matter what their grade.

Remember, a lifetime love of reading starts with a single step!

For my fabulous friend,
Fran Manushkin
—D.H.

Text copyright © 1998 by Deborah Hautzig. Illustrations copyright © 1998 by Sylvie Wickstrom. All rights reserved under International and Pan-American Copyright Conventions. Published in the United States by Random House Children's Books, a division of Random House, Inc., New York, and simultaneously in Canada by Random House of Canada Limited, Toronto.
www.stepintoreading.com
Educators and librarians, for a variety of teaching tools, visit us at
www.randomhouse.com/teachers
Library of Congress Cataloging-in-Publication Data
Hautzig, Deborah.   Little Witch goes to school / by Deborah Hautzig ; illustrated by Sylvie Wickstrom.
   p.   cm. — (Step into reading. A step 3 book.)
SUMMARY: Little Witch goes to school for the first time and takes her classmates on a broomstick ride.
ISBN 0-679-88738-5 (trade) — ISBN 0-679-98738-X (lib. bdg.)
[1. Witches—Fiction. 2. Schools—Fiction. 3. First day of school—Fiction.] I. Wickstrom, Sylvie, ill.
II. Title. III. Series: Step into reading. Step 3 book. PZ7.H2888 Ligf 2003 [E]—dc21 2002014814
Printed in the United States of America   26 25 24 23 22 21 20
STEP INTO READING, RANDOM HOUSE, and the Random House colophon are registered trademarks of Random House, Inc.

STEP INTO READING®

STEP 3

Little Witch Goes to School

By Deborah Hautzig

Illustrated by Sylvie Wickstrom

Random House New York

Little Witch was bored.

There was nobody to play with

except her cat, Bow-Wow,

and her bat, Scrubby.

And they were bored, too.

Little Witch went into the kitchen.

There was Mother Witch,

making spaghetti and mouseballs.

6 FAT
MICE

"There is nobody to play with,"
Little Witch told Mother Witch.
"Everybody is starting
school today—except me.
I'm *bored*. I miss my friends."
"Good!" said Mother Witch.
"I like it when you complain.

"Go find Aunt Nasty
and Aunt Grouchy.
Maybe they can
teach you to be mean."
"I'm not very good
at being mean,"
said Little Witch.
"Well, TRY HARDER!"
screamed Mother Witch.

Aunt Nasty was on the roof
with Aunt Grouchy.
They were throwing
smelly old eggs
at the mailman.
"You always bring JUNK!"
screamed Aunt Nasty.
Little Witch felt sorry
for him.

She said a magic spell:

"Soapy dopey,

Eggy free,

You're as clean

As clean can be!"

ZAP! The mailman was clean.

"Party pooper!"

shrieked Aunt Grouchy.

"Go away, Little Witch!"

Little Witch went
back inside.
"Aunt Grouchy told me to go away.
What can I do now,
Mother Witch?"
"Go find Cousin Dippy,"
said Mother Witch.
"She is always doing
something stupid.
Maybe you can help."

Cousin Dippy was in the yard.
"The leaves are
falling off the tree!
So I'm taping them back on."
"Cousin Dippy doesn't
understand about Fall,"
Little Witch whispered
to Bow-Wow.
"The leaves are *supposed*
to fall off."

Little Witch went

into the kitchen again.

"Can I *please* go to school?"

she begged.

"No! And NEVER say PLEASE!"

yelled Mother Witch.

"What if I promise to be good?"

asked Little Witch.

"You are ALREADY too good!"

screamed Mother Witch.

"Okay," said Little Witch quietly.

"What if I promise to be *bad?*"

Mother Witch looked up.

Her witchy eyes twinkled.

"Deal!" said Mother Witch.

The next morning,
Little Witch got ready for school.
Aunt Grouchy and Aunt Nasty
gave her a wormy apple
for the teacher.
Cousin Dippy gave her
a box of crayons.
Mother Witch gave her
a lunchbox full of candy.
"This will help your teeth rot,"
she said.

"Remember to be bad!

Don't make any new friends!

And DON'T LEARN ANYTHING!"

"I'll try, Mother Witch,"

said Little Witch.

"See you later, everybody!"

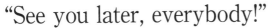

When Little Witch got to school,

she saw her friends

Milly, Sam, and Marcus.

"Here I am!" said Little Witch.

The teacher's name

was Ms. Brooks.

She was shocked to see

Little Witch in her classroom.

But she was very polite.

"We have a new student today,"

she told the class.

"Can you tell her your names?"

One by one, everyone

said their names.

"Why are you dressed

as a witch, dear?"

asked Ms. Brooks.

She looked worried.

"Because I *am* a witch,"

said Little Witch proudly.

"But there are no *real* witches,"

said Ms. Brooks.

"Oh, yes, there are!" cried Milly.

"Show her, Little Witch!"

So Little Witch said
a magic spell:
"Flippety dippety,
Witch's broom,
Watch me fly
Around this room!"

WHOOSH!
Little Witch flew
around and around
the classroom.

Ms. Brooks gasped.
She had never seen
a real witch before.
"That's amazing!" cried Cherry.
"Can you teach us to fly, too?"
"WHAT?" shrieked Ms. Brooks.

"Don't worry," said Little Witch.
"I will take everyone for a ride—
after school.
School is much more fun
than flying!"
Ms. Brooks was very relieved
to hear *that*.

"Here is an apple for you,

Ms. Brooks,"

said Little Witch.

Suddenly the worms popped out.

Ms. Brooks screamed.

"I'll fix it in a jiffy,"

said Little Witch.

She said these magic words:

"Junky monkey,

Stinkeroozer,

This old apple

Is a loser!"

POOF! The wormy apple

was gone.

In its place was a banana.

"I hope you like bananas,"

said Little Witch.

Little Witch looked

around the classroom.

Each child had a cubby

to put things in.

"This cubby is yours,"

Ms. Brooks told Little Witch.

"Wow," said Little Witch.

"I never had a cubby before."

"And I never had a little witch
in my class before!"
said Ms. Brooks.

"You do now,"
said Little Witch happily.

"Everyone sit in a circle,"
said Ms. Brooks.
"Whose job is it to
feed the fish today?"
"Cherry and Mary,"
said Marcus.
"They like to do things together,"
he told Little Witch.

"What will my job be?"
asked Little Witch.
"You may clean up
the floor after art class,"
said Ms. Brooks.
"Thank you!" cried Little Witch.
"I love to clean up!"

Art came next.

Ms. Brooks let everyone

draw pictures.

Little Witch used her crayons

from Cousin Dippy.

But something was not right.

"Oh, dear," said Little Witch.

"The blue one draws in green.

The green one draws in purple.

The yellow one draws in blue.

They're all mixed up—

just like Cousin Dippy."

"I'll trade you," said Willie.

"Your crayons are much

more fun."

"Deal!" said Little Witch.

"I always wanted real crayons."

When it was time to clean up,

Little Witch said

some magic words:

"Ickety stickety,

Messy floor,

You're as clean

As you were before!"

POOF! The floor was clean.

Everyone clapped—

even Ms. Brooks.

After art,

it was time to eat lunch.

"Look what Little Witch has

in her lunchbox!" cried Mary.

"It's candy!" cried Cherry.

"Yes," said Little Witch sadly.

"Mother Witch always

gives me candy for lunch."

"Let's trade," said Cherry.

"If you give us your candy,
  we will each give you
  half a sandwich."

"Deal!" said Little Witch happily.

"I never get a sandwich
  for lunch!"

After lunch came recess.
Ms. Brooks let everyone
play in the yard.
Cherry and Mary and Willie
and Walter showed Little Witch
how to play games
she had never played before.
They played hopscotch...and tag...
and hide-and-seek...
and Simon says.

In the afternoon,

Ms. Brooks read a story out loud.

It was about a tiny girl

named Thumbelina.

Then the children made up

their own story.

It was about a tiny boy

named Pinky.

Ms. Brooks wrote down the words.

"Tomorrow we can make

our own book," said Ms. Brooks.

"Great idea!" said Esther.

All the children agreed.

Then it was time to go home.

Little Witch was so sorry
that school was over!
She began to cry.
"Don't worry," said Ms. Brooks.
"You can come back tomorrow."
Little Witch stopped crying.
"I forgot about tomorrow.
I feel much better now.
Good-bye, everybody!"

"WAIT!" cried Cherry.

"You promised us a ride!"

"Oops! You're right,"

said Little Witch.

"But first, we need

an extra-long broomstick."

Little Witch said:

"Roomy broomy,

Stringy cheese,

I need a ten-foot

Broomstick, please!"

In a flash,

she was holding

the longest broomstick ever.

"Hop on!" said Little Witch.

"Now we need a flying spell,"
said Little Witch.
She said:
  "Twinkle dinkle,
  Frenchy fry,
  Now we're flying
  In the sky!"

With a loud WHOOSH,

they took off.

They flew over towns

and around tall buildings...

They flew over the ocean...

They flew all the way to Paris....

And then they flew

over and under

London Bridge!

At last—THUMP!

They landed in front of

Little Witch's house.

There was Mother Witch,

waiting on the porch.

"Who are all these children?"

said Mother Witch.

"These are my friends

from school!"

said Little Witch.

"I TOLD you not to
make any friends!"
screamed Mother Witch.
"Send them home,
and GO TO BED!"
Little Witch said a spell:
"Snuggly wuggly,
Sleepyheads,
Zap my friends
Into their beds."
POOF! Her friends were gone.
Little Witch felt very sad.

Mother Witch came into

Little Witch's room.

Little Witch hid under the covers.

"You broke your promise,"

said Mother Witch.

"I know," said Little Witch.

"It's *bad* to break a promise,"

said Mother Witch.

"I know," said Little Witch.

Then Mother Witch smiled
and said, "You see?
You were bad after all!
I'm proud of you,
Little Witch."

Mother Witch hugged Little Witch.

"Good night," said Mother Witch.

"I hope you have
lots of bad dreams."
But Little Witch
had good dreams all night
about her wonderful day
at school.